BILLY AND THE MINI MONSTERS

Monsters to the Rescue

ZANNA DAVIDSON

Illustrated by
MELANIE WILLIAMSON

Reading consultant: Alison Kelly

Meet Billy...

Billy was just an ordinary boy living an ordinary life, until **ONE NIGHT** he found five **MINI MONSTERS** in his sock drawer.

Gloop   Peep   Fang-Face   Captain Snott   Trumpet

Then he saved their lives, and they swore never to leave him.

We give you the Secret-Hairy-Snot-Tooth Oath of Devotion.

We're awesome!

And fun!

And SCARY!

Are we scary? I'm not sure I'm very scary.

One thing was certain — Billy's life would never be the same **AGAIN**...

Contents

Chapter 1
Miserable Mondays

Billy was feeling fed up. It was Monday and that meant swimming lessons.

Mondays are miserable.

Billy **HATED** swimming lessons.

The Mini Monsters were doing everything they could to cheer him up.

Gloop did his eyeball trick.

Ta da!

Captain Snott sang his favorite song.

Happy Snottday to you, Happy Snottday to you...

Trumpet offered Billy a piece of (slightly moldy) cheese.

But nothing seemed to work.

"I don't like the way the water goes **up my nose**."

"And down my ears," said Billy.

"Or the way my hair always gets stuck in my swimming cap."

"But worst of all, I'm **TERRIBLE** at it. Last week, Mr. Roberts said I swam like a crazy monkey."

"And today there's going to be a diving competition. All the moms and dads are coming. But I can't

j

U

m

P

off a diving board."

"No way!" said Billy. "That would be a **DISASTER**."

The Mini Monsters were ALWAYS getting into trouble. Billy could just imagine what would happen if they came to the pool…

Gloop being sucked down a drain.

Peep getting lost in the lockers.

Captain Snott showing off.

Fang-Face getting stuck.

Trumpet disappearing on a cheese hunt.

Cheese!

13

"What I need," said Billy, "is a plan to get out of swimming."

PLAN TO GET OUT OF SWIMMING

1. Hide swimming things.

2. Cover face in green spots.

Unfortunately, his mom didn't fall for it…

"Come on," she said, taking Billy by the hand. "Your sister and I will be there cheering you on. It will all be fine."

17

18

19

20

21

Chapter 2
Into the Pool

Everyone else seemed really **excited** about the diving competition.

"I bet I do come last," thought Billy. **Meanwhile...**

...the Mini Monsters crept into Billy's locker to go over their plan.

"Quickly," said Captain Snott.
"Remember the plan…"

MAKE BILLY A SWIMMING
SUPERSTAR PLAN

1. Climb up to the
highest diving board.

2. Get Billy
to join us.

3. Help Billy to
jump off the
diving board.

4. Billy wins the diving
competition with our help!

As soon as he got into the pool, Billy looked up at the diving boards. They were completely **TERRIFYING.**

"We'll have our lesson first," said Mr. Roberts, the swimming teacher, "then it'll be time for the competition."

"And there's a race going on in the lanes," Mr. Roberts went on. "So whatever you do, keep to **this area** of the pool."

30

Chapter 3
Overboard!

Billy tried to listen to Mr. Roberts, but his eyes kept flicking towards the highest diving board.

Every time he saw it, he got a
WORRIED feeling in his tummy.

He wished
he had wings,
like Peep…

…or a cape,
like Captain
Snott…

…or **stretchy**
powers, like
Gloop.

"That's funny," thought Billy, looking across the pool, "I'm thinking about the Mini Monsters so much…"

…I can actually see them.

Billy rubbed his eyes and looked again. No, he realized, those *were* the Mini Monsters.

Billy was staring at them so hard he forgot to swim.

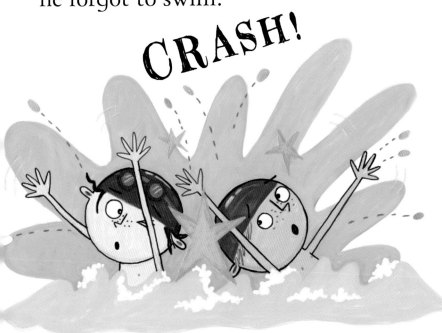

Then, to Billy's horror, a huge wave came… and knocked the Mini Monsters overboard.

One moment they were
on the floats…
the next,
they were

GONE!

Billy swam faster than he ever had before – straight through one racing lane...

...and then another.

Mr. Roberts was looking furious. And amazed.

But Billy didn't have time to stop.

"Got you!" said Billy, snatching the Mini Monsters out of the water.

Captain Snott looked around.

"**Oh no!**" he cried. "Where's Gloop?"

That's when the Mini Monsters saw Gloop. He was at the bottom of the pool being sucked down the drain!

41

44

Chapter 4
The Competition

Mr. Roberts came storming over. "What were you doing, Billy?"

"We'll have to talk about it later," his swimming teacher went on.

The competition is about to start.

Billy followed Mr. Roberts to the diving pool.

He joined the other children on the benches. He could see his mom waving at him.

One by one,

all the other
boys and girls

jumped off
the boards.

Even the best, bravest swimmers
didn't make it to the top one.

At last it was Billy's turn. "I'll just hold my nose and shut my eyes," he told himself.

But as he walked past the high board he looked up. To his **HORROR**, there were the Mini Monsters. Climbing up the ladder.

The plan is working brilliantly.

I can't believe the Mini Monsters are making me do this...

Billy knew he had to get them back.

He doesn't look very happy...

Billy gritted his teeth as he made his way to the top.

I'll get the Mini Monsters and climb straight back down.

There were gasps from the crowd as Billy stepped out onto the highest board.

Billy reached down to pick up the
Mini Monsters. But Gloop had left
a trail of slime behind him.
Billy slipped...

Whoooah!

...and wobbled...

...and slid right
to the end of the
diving board.

Aaargh!

For a moment, he stood looking down at the water. It seemed very far away.

Billy could hear cheers from the Mini Monsters behind him.

Billy shut his eyes, took a deep breath, and ju**mp**e*d*...

61

Chapter 5
Champion!

Billy landed in the water
with a **SPLASH!**

He could hear tiny splashes as the Mini Monsters landed beside him.

I really did it!

I did it!

Mr. Roberts came rushing over.
"Billy! How amazing! You've won
first prize!"

Billy couldn't believe it either.

He stood on the top of the
podium and was given a gold
medal and a trophy.

Back in the changing rooms, the Mini Monsters were celebrating, too.

"But where's Trumpet? And Peep?" asked Billy.

"Trumpet went to find some cheese," said Captain Snott. "And Peep went after him."

We all dived off the board!

I want to do it again!

After Billy had changed, everyone wanted to congratulate him.

But Billy was busy trying to figure out where Peep and Trumpet could have gone...

"I'd like to buy you a treat," said his mom, "for doing so well. Should we go for something special? What would you like?"

"That's it!" Billy realized suddenly. "The snack machine!"

Trumpet was always near food. He had to be *inside* the snack machine. Especially if it sold anything with CHEESE in it.

72

Chapter 6
Monster Competition

"Great job," said Billy's mom, on the way home. "I was so proud of you."

I knew you could do it. You're a swimming star.

As soon as Billy got home, he
rushed up to his room.

"That was amazing!" he said,
looking at the
Mini Monsters.

Let's
celebrate...

All about the
MINI MONSTERS

FANG-FACE

LIKES EATING:
socks, school ties,
paper, or anything
that comes his way.

SPECIAL SKILL:
has massive fangs.

SCARE FACTOR:
9/10

GLOOP

LIKES EATING: cake.

SPECIAL SKILL:
very stre-e-e-tchy.
Gloop can also swallow
his own eyeballs and
make them reappear on
any part of his body.

SCARE FACTOR:
4/10

CAPTAIN SNOTT

LIKES EATING: boogeys.

SPECIAL SKILL:
can glow in the dark.

**SCARE FACTOR:
5/10**

PEEP

LIKES EATING: very small flies.

SPECIAL SKILL: can fly (but not very far, or very well).

**SCARE FACTOR:
0/10** (unless you're afraid of small hairy things)

TRUMPET

LIKES EATING: cheese.

SPECIAL SKILL:
amazingly powerful
cheese-powered toots.

**SCARE FACTOR:
7/10**
(taking into
account his toots)

Edited by Lesley Sims and Becky Walker
Designed by Brenda Cole
Cover design by Hannah Cobley

Digital Manipulation by John Russell

First published in 2017 by Usborne Publishing Ltd., Usborne House,
83-85 Saffron Hill, London EC1N 8RT, England. www.usborne.com
Copyright © 2017 Usborne Publishing Ltd. AE